W9-BPL-542

Offen, Hilda
Good Girl, Gracie Growler

For Lydia

For a free color catalog describing Gareth Stevens Publishing's list of high-quality books and multimedia programs, call 1-800-542-2595 (USA) or 1-800-461-9120 (Canada). Gareth Stevens Publishing's Fax: (414) 225-0377. See our catalog, too, on the World Wide Web: http://gsinc.com

Library of Congress Cataloging-in-Publication Data
Offen, Hilda.
Good girl, Gracie Growler! / by Hilda Offen.
p. cm.
"First published in Great Britain in 1995 by Hamish Hamilton Ltd."--Imprint p.
Summary: Although Gracie's new baby brother gets a great deal of attention from the adults, she finds that he is giving her all of his attention.
ISBN 0-8368-1624-2 (lib. bdg.)
[1. Tigers--Fiction. 2. Babies--Fiction. 3. Brothers and sisters--
Fiction. 4. Sibling rivalry--Fiction.] I. Title.
PZ7.0327Go 1996
[E]--dc20 96-31212

First published in North America in 1996 by
Gareth Stevens Publishing
1555 North RiverCenter Drive, Suite 201
Milwaukee, Wisconsin 53212 USA

Text and illustrations © 1995 by Hilda Offen. First published in Great Britain in 1995 by Hamish Hamilton Ltd. The moral right of the author has been asserted.

Printed in the United States of America

1 2 3 4 5 6 7 8 9 00 99 98 97 96

GOOD GIRL,
GRACIE GROWLER!

Hilda Offen

Gareth Stevens Publishing
MILWAUKEE

"Meet your new brother, Gracie!" said Mrs. Growler.
"His name's Tommy."
"Would you like to give him a present?" asked Mr. Growler.
"Yes," said Gracie. "He can have my rabbit."

Mr. and Mrs. Growler loved their baby.
"See how tiny his toes are!" said Mr. Growler.
"Careful, Gracie!" said Mrs. Growler.
"You're stepping on Tommy's rattle!"

The Growlers watched the baby all the time.
"What dear little whiskers he has!" said Mrs. Growler.
"Oh — look!" said Mr. Growler.
"He's smiling! It's his very first smile!"

One morning, the baby stopped smiling and started to cry.
He howled and howled and howled.
"We'll take him for a walk," said Mrs. Growler.

"Look at me!" called Gracie.
"Ssh!" said Mrs. Growler. "Tommy's settling down —
you'll start him off again."

11

Suddenly, the baby opened his mouth
as wide as he could. "He's trying to show
us something!" said Mr. Growler.

"It's his first tooth!" cried Mrs. Growler.
"Tommy's got his first tooth!"
"What a clever young man!" said Mr. Growler.

Not long after this, Grandma Growler came to visit.
"Look what I can do, Gran!" said Gracie.
"Very nice, dear!" said Gran. "Now — where's my best boy?"

"He's over there," said Gracie.
"Tommy!" called Gran. "Give your Grandma a hug!"
She hugged the baby and kissed him on the nose.

"Come in, and have a cup of tea," said Mr. Growler.
Grandma put Tommy down on the carpet.
"He's so sweet!" she said.

All at once, the baby shot forward.
"Just look at that!" said Mr. Growler.
"Our Tommy's learned to crawl!"
"Well done, Tommy!" they said. "You clever, *clever* boy!"

People were always coming around to see the baby.
One summer's day, Mr. and Mrs. Lion
strolled up the garden path.

18

"Auntie Rose! Uncle Joe!" called Gracie.
"See what I've learned to do!" "Good for you, Gracie!"
they said. "Where's your little brother?
We've brought him a jumpsuit."

The Lions watched while Mrs. Growler
dressed the baby in his new outfit.
"What a handsome child!" said Mrs. Lion.
Tommy stood up. He lifted one foot — then another.

"Would you believe it?" cried Mrs. Growler.
"Our Tommy's learned to walk!"
Everyone started to clap.
"Hip-hip-hooray!" they shouted.

While they were clapping and cheering,
the baby opened his mouth.
"He spoke!" gasped Mrs. Growler.
"Tommy spoke! I think he said 'Mom.'"

"No, dearest, he said 'Dad,'" said Mr. Growler.
"I thought he said 'Auntie Rose,'" said Auntie Rose.
"It was definitely 'Uncle Joe,'" said Uncle Joe.
But Gracie heard what Tommy really said.

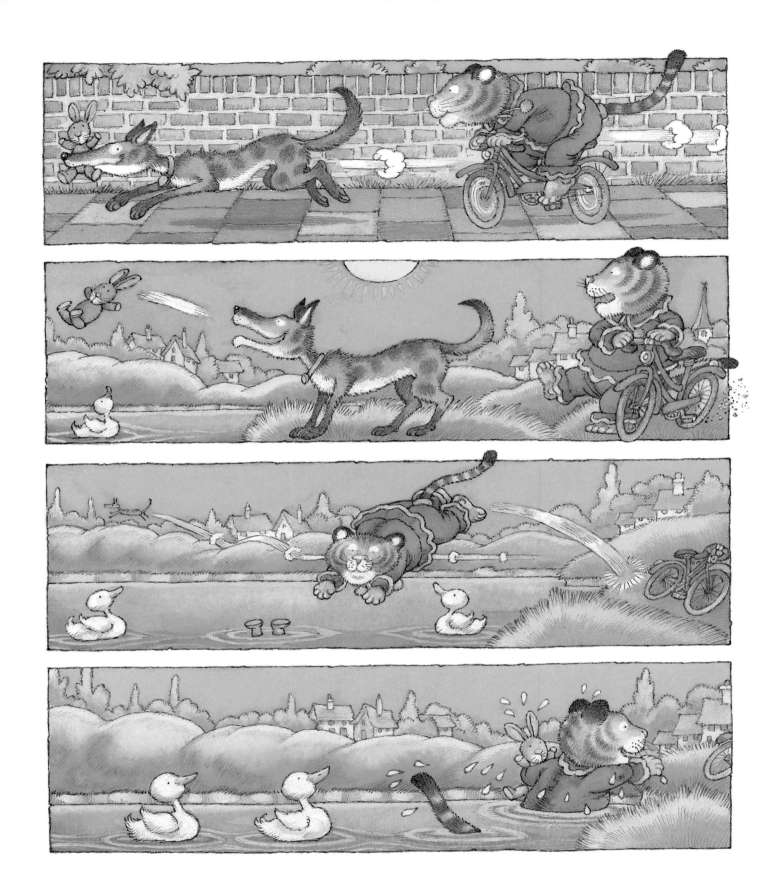

She jumped on her bike and rode away down the street to the park. There was a lot to do before she could go home!

As she cycled back through the gate,
the baby shouted loudly.
This time everyone heard what he said.
There was no mistake about it!
"GRACIE!" yelled Baby Tommy.

The grown-ups stared in surprise.
"Gracie walks on walls!" shouted the baby.
"Gracie walks on clotheslines! Gracie rides upside-down
on bikes! Gracie does tricks on swings!"

"Well, I never!" said Mr. Growler.
"Can you really do all those things, Gracie?"
"GRACIE RESCUED MY RABBIT!" roared the baby.

"Good heavens!" said Mr. and Mrs. Growler.
They gave Gracie a great big hug.
"You clever girl!" they said.
"You good, *good* girl! Well done!"

"Gracie! Gracie!" shouted the baby.
"I want Gracie!" Gracie took his hand.
"Come on, Tommy," she said.
"I'll teach you how to walk on walls!"

29